SAM PARROW AND THE TIME STONE SECRET

Sam's 3rd exciting time travel adventure

Gill Parkes

Copyright © 2021 Gill Parkes

All rights reserved

ISBN: 9798520163909
Imprint: Independently published

Cover design by: Art Painter
Library of Congress Control Number: 2018675309
Printed in the United States of America

*For Martin, for all your support and encourage-
ment. I couldn't have done it without you!*

"I will tell of the Lord's unfailing love. I will praise the Lord for all he has done. I will rejoice in his great goodness to Israel, which he has granted according to his mercy and love. He said,
"They are my very own people. Surely they will not betray me again."
And he became their Saviour.
In all their suffering he also suffered, and he personally rescued them.
In his love and mercy he redeemed them. He lifted them up and carried them through all the years."

ISAIAH 63 VS 7-9 (NEW LIVING TRANSLATION)

CONTENTS

MAP OF ISRAEL

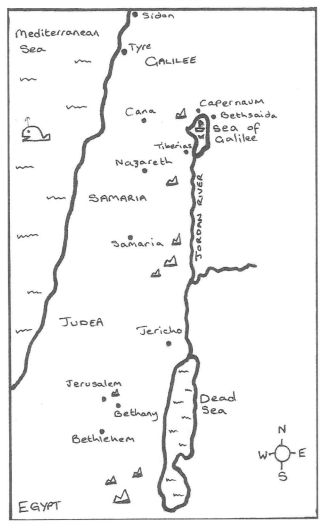

TEMPLE PLAN

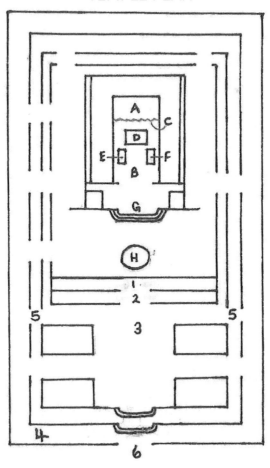

KEY

1 Hall of Priests
2 Hall of Israelites
3 Court of the Women
4 Court of the Gentiles
5 Womens' Gate
6 East Gate
A Holy of Holies

B Holy Place
C Curtain
D Incense Altar
E Candlestick
F Table of Shewbread
G 12 Steps
H Brazen Altar

LIST OF CHARACTERS

Alex, Ben & Jamie - *Sam's friends, 21st century*

Chris - *Youth group leader*

Daniel (Belteshazzar) - *Captured prince of Judah*

Dayle & Kate - *Sam's friends, 21st century*

Eli & Dinah - *Matthew's uncle & aunt*

Elisha - *A prophet*

Gehazi - *Elisha's servant*

Hepzibah - *the goat*

Lame man & friends - *seekers of Jesus*

Leper - *grateful man*

Matthew - *Sam's friend, 1st century*

Naaman - *Soldier in need of healing*

Nebuchadnezzar - *King of Babylon*

Older Rachel - *Matthew's mum*

Ollie & Jack - *School bullies*

Peter - *Jesus' friend*

Pharisees - *Lawmakers*

Sam - *12-year-old time traveller*

Shadrach, Meshach & Abednego - *Daniel's friends*

Simon, Adah & Hanani - *Rachel's son & family*

Solomon - *3rd King of Israel*

Uzziah - *10th King of Judah*

Young Rachel - *Sam's friend, 1st century*

CHAPTER 1

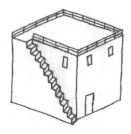

Sam stretched and watched the dust motes dancing in the sunlight that streamed in through the small window near the ceiling. The mattress next to his was empty indicating that his friend Matthew was already up. Getting out of bed, he dressed in a knee-length woollen tunic like those worn by boys in ancient Israel. He tied a rope belt around his middle and made sure that the leather pouch containing his precious stone was safely attached. Sam went down the steps to the day room, bare feet on cold stone. Bowls of fruit and yoghurt were waiting on the table so he sat down to eat. He wondered where Matthew and his mother, Rachel, had got to.

Sam had first met Rachel as a young girl when the time stone had brought him back in time to Bethlehem. At that time she was a shepherdess, helping her brothers care for their sheep. Sam had met her again thirty years later when he bumped into her son when the time stone had taken him to Jericho. It had been a shock to see the young girl he had first met on a hillside in Bethlehem was not only older, but she had five children and was also a grandmother! Since that first meeting, they had shared many adventures, visiting events from the past and learning about God's love along the way.

Sam had found the stone while on holiday in Norfolk. At first, he thought it was just a broken piece from a small cross but that night, with a flash of blue light, it had transported him back in time to witness events that had changed his life forever.

His last adventure though, to the time of King Nebuchadnezzar of Babylon, had upset him and he had been grateful that he had been with the older Rachel who had cared for him as though he was her son. Finishing his breakfast, Sam washed his bowl then put on his leather sandals that were waiting by the door and went outside to look for his friends. Rachel was milking the goat which was happily occupied eating anything within reach but Matthew was nowhere in sight. Sam stood in the doorway and thought how different life was here to the life he had in England, almost two thousand years in the future. He enjoyed his visits but he was always glad to go home in between!

Rachel stood up and patted the goat, murmuring soothing words to her as she scratched the goat's ears. Picking up the pail, she carried it over to the house where she saw Sam watching her.

"Sam, you're up!" she said, placing the pail of fresh creamy milk inside the house to keep cool. "Have you eaten?"

"Yes thank you. Where's Matthew?"

"I sent him to take a message to my brother, Eli. He'll be back soon."

"I remember him from the first time we met! He was so happy to see baby Jesus."

"Yes, but not so happy now. His wife is ill so I sent Matthew to say I will visit later with a meal for them. Come, let's sit outside and talk about our latest adventure."

A fig tree grew in one corner of the courtyard providing much-needed shade from the hot sun. Rachel and Sam sat underneath and leant against the trunk. They had just got comfortable when Matthew came in through the gate.

"Matthew come and join us," called his mother, "Sam and I were just going to talk about our latest adventure!"

"Oh good, Ima told me you went to Babylon last night!" Matthew said to Sam as he sat down in front of him, "I wish I'd gone with you."

"I'm sorry. The stone had taken me home first but then it brought me back again to the time when we had just gone to bed after the party. You'd gone to sleep as soon as your head hit the pillow but I'd been home for a week so I was no longer tired!"

Matthew grinned, "It's all right, I know you have no control over the stone. Tell me about your trip."

Sam pulled a face, "I didn't like the start of it much, it was horrific! It ended well though."

Rachel nodded, "We saw the three young men, Shadrach, Meshach and Abednego thrown into the fiery furnace! I'm afraid it was a story that Sam hadn't heard before and he was a little upset."

"I couldn't believe how cruel that king was. He

didn't even care that his guards were killed when they got too close to the fire!"

"I know Sam. Sadly some people can only show how great they are by being cruel to others. They think that it shows their superiority if people are afraid of them. In reality, they are often afraid themselves and use their power to stop people seeing the truth."

Sam thought about Ollie and Jack, the two boys at school who seemed to enjoy bullying him at every opportunity. He wondered what they were afraid of - probably of losing to someone like him, not that that was ever likely to happen.

"But the men got out didn't they, Yahweh saved them!" declared Matthew, dragging Sam's attention back to the first century.

"Yes, it was awesome!" agreed Sam, "They weren't hurt at all!"

Rachel smiled, "That's right, they did what was right and refused to worship the idol that the king had ordered to be made. Yahweh says we should only worship him and if we are obedient he will always help us."

"So did the king worship Yahweh after that, when he saw how he had looked after the men in the fire?" Sam asked her.

"Not then, Nebuchadnezzar was very proud so a few more things had to happen first, but he did worship him in the end."

A low humming sound came from the leather pouch hanging from Sam's belt. He grinned at his two friends. Each of them felt excited as all three wondered where, and when, their next adventure would be.

"Hold on!" said Sam as he removed the time stone and held it firmly in his hand. As the hum got louder the stone began to glow, lighting up the courtyard with its strange blue light. In a flash the scene changed, the courtyard disappeared and the three friends found themselves inside the walls of a great city.

CHAPTER 2

"Where are we?" asked Matthew and Sam together. The boys laughed and looked at Rachel who said, "And when are we?"

"Ima your hair is different, you have curls!" exclaimed Matthew.

"Oh my goodness!" Rachel put her hand up to her hair and felt the ringlets that hung down over her shoulders. "Our clothes are different too, we all have colourful shawls with tassels over our tunics."

"They only go over one shoulder though, more like a wide sash," said Sam, adjusting the wide leather belt that held the shawl together at his waist. He noticed that he still had a pouch so he put the time stone inside to keep it safe.

They looked around at the beautiful white stone

buildings that surrounded the square where they were standing. In front of them, steps led up to an impressive looking building with people going up and down looking important. Small groups of men stood talking together in the shade of the portico at the top. Rather like a huge porch at the entrance, it had four tall pillars along each side holding up an ornate roof. Just then, four young men passed in front of them, walking towards the steps.

Sam gasped, "Aren't they Shadrach, Meshach and Abednego? I wonder who the fourth one is."

"Do you think it could be Daniel, Ima?"

"Boys hush, they'll hear you!" Rachel frowned, she wouldn't know what to say if anyone questioned who they were. "He could be Daniel, although he is called Belteshazzar here, the four of them were good friends. They look quite young though and not so richly dressed. I think we may have arrived earlier than before."

The young man they were talking about turned and walked back to speak to Rachel.

"Shalom," he said, "do I know you? I heard you speak my Hebrew name, are you from Jerusalem?"

Rachel hesitated, "Shalom, erm no, we are from Bethlehem."

Daniel looked puzzled, "Yet you seem to know who we are. You are not dressed as slaves and your sons are not a part of the group set aside to serve in the royal palace. May I ask who you are?"

"My name is Rachel and the boys are Matthew and Samuel."

Daniel smiled, "I am pleased to meet you. We are going back to our living quarters, perhaps you would like to join us? It would be good to hear news from home."

Unsure what to do, Rachel decided that the stone always had a reason for taking them to the places it did so she agreed.

"Thank you, we would like that."

The three friends followed the four young men up the steps into the entrance to the royal palace. At the top, they turned left and Daniel led them to a large courtyard where groups of young men were sat talking. He chose two benches that were next to a table, set apart from the nearest group.

"Please sit, we will not be overheard here so we can speak freely."

Sam was relieved, he wasn't at all sure that anything he had to say would be very welcome. He remembered what twelve-year-old Rachel had said

14

about him being thought of as a sorcerer if her brothers found out about the time stone. When he had got home after that visit he had looked on the internet to find out what the elders did to people accused of sorcery and witchcraft. Having rocks and stones thrown at him until he was dead was something he could well do without.

"Is this your school?" asked Matthew looking around at the different groups, some of whom seemed to be having heated discussions.

"Yes," answered Meshach, "we have been brought here to learn the language and culture of Babylon."

Shadrach nodded, "We have all been chosen by the king to serve him in the palace but first we must prove our worth."

"Belteshazzar has certainly done that," grinned Abednego, "he's our top student!"

Daniel smiled, "I do only what Yahweh tells me to do and he rewards me with his wisdom."

"You boys are highly favoured," agreed Rachel, "Yahweh honours those who keep his commands."

"Indeed he does my lady but I am curious. Why has Yahweh brought you to us?" Daniel looked at Rachel kindly, treating her with the respect that Yahweh expected from him for someone older.

"I'm not sure," she said, "although if your language skills are good you may be able to help us." Rachel turned to Sam, "Samuel, perhaps we should show them your stone?"

Sam looked at Rachel, horrified. Did she really think that was a good idea? Daniel smiled encouragingly, sensing that something was troubling him.

"It's all right, you are safe here, you won't come to any harm."

Not entirely believing him, Sam carefully took out the time stone and placed it on the table in front of them.

"We were wondering what the symbols mean," he said. Daniel picked it up and studied the symbols carved in the stone.

"What do you think? It looks a little like Hebrew script," he said, passing it to his friends. Abednego took the stone and turned it over, looking for anything that might help with its translation.

"Where did you find it?" he asked. Sam looked at Rachel, wide-eyed with fear. This whole thing of time travel sounded so impossible, even to him! Thankfully, Rachel could see how he was feeling and spoke up.

"Samuel found it at home," she said, which was

as near to the truth as any of them were willing to go.

Meshach peered at the stone before passing it on to Shadrach.

"The symbols have several meanings, dalet at the top represents a door and means 'entrance' or 'movement'," he said, "And ayin, the eye, could mean 'to watch' or 'know'."

Shadrach looked up at the three strangers in front of him, "Reading the symbols is the easy part, interpreting their meaning can be more difficult." He turned to Daniel, "You are best at interpretation. Perhaps we should leave you to study it alone."

"Good idea, Shadrach," agreed Abednego, "we have work to do. Our studies don't come quite so easily to us!" The four young men laughed as Shadrach, Meshach and Abednego stood up to leave.

"Forgive us for not staying my lady," bowed Meshach, "but Belteshazzar is indeed more able to help you. Perhaps we will meet again."

Sam watched the three young men cross the courtyard and enter the building. He was strangely relieved that there was only Daniel left, he felt safer somehow.

"I think I would like to hear your story," smiled Daniel. Rachel, Matthew and Sam looked at each other, wondering how much of their story to share. When Sam had first told Rachel the truth she had had to believe him because the stone had taken both of them back in time to watch David defeat Goliath. Now though, it didn't look as if the stone was taking them anywhere else until Daniel had solved the mystery of the symbols. Taking a deep breath, Sam picked up the stone and said to Daniel,

"We're from the future."

CHAPTER 3

Daniel looked at the three friends sat in front of him. Neither Rachel nor Matthew had disagreed with Samuel's outrageous claim. If he was telling the truth it would explain why they were so reluctant to share their story.

"How did you get here?" he asked, "And where have you come from?"

"We have come from Bethlehem, as I told you," said Rachel, "but we have come from many years in the future."

"I find that very hard to believe. You must agree that what you say is impossible."

Rachel smiled, "The first time I met Samuel we travelled back in time to when David slew Goliath. If I hadn't experienced it myself I would have agreed with you."

"These are not your sons?"

"Matthew is but I first met Samuel when I was a young girl and we had many adventures together. We met again more recently. Though I have grown older, Samuel is still the age that we first met."

Daniel looked baffled, "That must seem very strange," he said.

"Totally," agreed Sam, "The whole thing is really weird, but it's still true."

"Ima and I both believe that Samuel has come to us to learn about Yahweh. He knew nothing of him in the beginning," joined in Matthew.

"Yes, and I've learnt a lot!"

Rachel laughed, "You certainly have, I'm sure Yahweh is very pleased with you."

Sam blushed, he didn't like being the centre of attention, he would prefer it if they got back to the writing on the stone.

"We know it's hard for you to believe, but maybe the writing will help," he said.

"You still haven't told me how you came to be here."

Sam sighed and explained how he had found the stone in the sand and how it had begun to hum when he was in bed that night. He told Daniel about the strange blue light that came from it when he picked it up and how he had suddenly found himself on a hillside in Bethlehem.

"It made me feel sick and dizzy," he said, "although I've got used to it now so it's not so bad."

Daniel picked up the stone and turned it over, "Apart from the writing there is nothing to distinguish it from any other stone."

"No, but perhaps the writing will explain it," Sam looked hopefully at Daniel, "Please, can you tell us what it says?"

Daniel studied the symbols. He still didn't quite believe what they had told him but he knew that there were many strange things in the world. Perhaps this was just another one of them. He frowned, now that he had heard their story the writing did make more sense.

"Each symbol represents an idea and we find their meaning by looking at them together. Look at this one near the top, it looks like the sun on the horizon. Its name is quph and it can mean 'circle' or 'time'. This one next to it, tsade, looks like a trail and means 'chase' or 'a journey'. Therefore, if you are telling the truth, we can read them as a journey through time."

"So the symbols are important," said Rachel.

"Yes, if we look at the symbols underneath,

lamed and hey, we see the purpose of the journey. Lamed looks like a shepherds staff, it means 'teach' or 'toward'. Hey represents a man with arms raised to heaven and means 'behold' or 'revelation' because the raised arms are pointing towards a great sight that should not be missed."

"Wow!" Sam was impressed with Daniel's ability to make sense of the symbols, "Have you learnt this while you've been here?"

"No, I was taught this as a child when I lived in Jerusalem. I'm surprised you don't know it your-selves if you are from Bethlehem. It is Hebrew script."

Matthew shook his head, "This is not the script we are taught. The symbols are different."

"No it isn't," agreed Rachel, "I believe the lan-guage is the same although it is only spoken when we read the Torah, our people speak Aramaic now. I think the way we write it has changed though."

"Meshach said the eye means to watch or know," said Sam, keen to bring the conversation back to the translation.

"Yes and next to it is gimel which represents a foot and means 'to walk'. So if we put them all to-gether we can understand the story that is written on the stone."

"What about the ones at the top and bottom?" asked Sam.

"At the top is dalet, as Meshach has already explained. It means 'door' or 'entrance'. The one at the bottom is samech. This one is more difficult to interpret as it shows a thorn and has meanings that seem to oppose each other." Daniel paused to think about what he could see, "I think the correct meaning here would be 'protect'."

Rachel nodded thoughtfully, "So the stone is the entrance for travelling through time?"

"That's right and its purpose is to teach the traveller by showing him important events that will bring greater knowledge and understanding. The symbol at the bottom suggests that the traveller will be safe from harm."

Sam breathed a sigh of relief. Maybe he wouldn't get stoned for sorcery after all! "So do you believe us now?" he asked.

"I think that I don't disbelieve you, but it is still an incredible story that you have shared."

"Well, at least we know what the writing says now," Matthew picked up the stone and looked at the symbols again, "I suppose some of them are similar to the script we use, although none are exactly the same."

"How far ahead in time have you come from?"

"Probably about six hundred years," said Rachel deciding that Daniel didn't need to know that Sam lived even further ahead in time.

"And is Israel free in your time?"

"Israel has seen many changes and will undoubtedly see many more, but it still exists as a nation." Rachel was careful not to say anything that would influence Daniel in any way. "King Solomon wrote that no man knows the future. I believe that Yahweh would not want us to tell you anymore. I'm sorry, Daniel."

"We have only ever travelled backwards in time. We've never gone into any future except our own." Sam looked at Daniel, willing him to believe them.

"That's right, I would love to visit Samuel's home but the stone always takes him back when he is alone." Matthew grinned, "It's probably just as well, I'm not sure I would want to see a world that knows so little about Yahweh!"

Daniel looked at the three friends sitting opposite him. Their story was hard to believe but the writing on the stone was quite definite. He smiled, no one knows the mind of Yahweh, his thoughts are not the same as those of man. If this was how he chose to teach the boy about himself who were they to question it?

"It is not for me to question the ways of God," he said, "and if it truly was he that brought you here I am glad to have been able to help."

"Thank you, Daniel, you have solved a great mystery for us," smiled Rachel, "May Yahweh reward your generosity."

"Thank you, my lady, and now I fear I must leave you. My friends are not the only ones who need to study." Daniel stood up to leave and bowed his head politely, "Shalom, perhaps Yahweh will allow us to meet again."

As Daniel left to go inside, the three friends realised that they were alone. All the other groups of young men had gone, leaving the courtyard deserted. As if it knew this was an ideal opportunity, the stone hummed, glowed and whisked them away.

In the palace courtyard, Daniel turned around to take another look at the three strangers from Bethlehem. He was surprised to see the courtyard was empty - the three strangers had disappeared.

CHAPTER 4

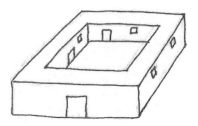

"Well! That was interesting," said Rachel as they arrived with a bump, back under the fig tree.

"I'm glad we know what the symbols mean now. If I'd been able to read them in the beginning I might not have been so surprised the first time I came to Bethlehem!"

"Really?" asked Matthew, "Do you know of others who have travelled through time then?"

"No, it's not something anyone really believes is possible but it is something that a lot of people would like to do. There's a lot of TV, er, I mean stories, about it." Sam had been about to say TV programmes but stopped himself just in time. He had no idea how he would explain television to them!

"I suppose you two are hungry?" Rachel looked

at the boys who grinned sheepishly at her.

"Did you really need to ask?" said Matthew, hugging his mother, "It's been a long time since breakfast!"

After feasting on bread, cheese and olives, Rachel told them she needed to prepare a meal for her brother so she sent them outside out of her way. The boys went back to sit under the tree and Sam asked about Matthew's brother and sisters.

"Simon lives with us with his wife, Adah and their son Hanani. He's almost two and terrorises the hens! Adah has just learnt she's having another baby so she's taken Hanani to visit her mother. They live in Jerusalem so we'll meet with them for Passover and then she'll come back with us."

"Don't you have three sisters too?"

"Yes, they all live with their husband's families. That's our custom, Ima came to live with Abba's family when she married. This house used to belong to Saba and Savta. Who do you live with?"

"Oh there are only my parents and me at home," answered Sam, "I don't have any brothers or sisters and my grandparents live in their own home nearby." Sam thought it would be good to be a part of a big family, even if it did mean less space in the house, "I'd like to meet your family," he added wistfully.

"Perhaps the stone will bring you back for Passover so you can. I'm not sure how we'll explain you though!"

The two boys laughed at the thought of trying to explain how Sam came to be in Bethlehem when the stone began to hum.

"I wonder where we'll go this time," said Sam as the stone glowed and took them back in time.

The two boys were standing in the street outside a very crowded house. Sam wrinkled his nose, "I smell fish! I suppose we're in Capernaum again."

"Yes and I suppose that Jesus is inside the house which is why there are so many people here!"

"There's no way we can get inside," said Sam, "We can't even get through the door."

"No and they don't stand much chance either," agreed Matthew, looking at a group of men, some of whom carried another man who was lying on a mat. The two boys watched to see what they would do. Finding that there was no way in, two of the men carefully carried their friend up the stone steps that ran up the outside of the house.

"Come on, let's go with them," said Matthew, pulling Sam towards the steps. The boys followed the men onto the flat roof and watched as they gently lay their friend down. The friends then started to dig through the hardened mud that formed the roof, creating an opening into the room below. The house was a single storey, like the one in Jericho, so the opening led into the room where Jesus was speaking.

Matthew and Sam edged closer so that they could see what was happening. Four of the men took a corner of the mat each and lowered him through the hole in the roof. The mat, with the man on it, landed right in front of Jesus. The friends knelt around the hole, leaning over to watch what would happen. Matthew and Sam joined them, not wanting to miss the chance of seeing another miracle. They recognised Peter, one of Jesus' disciples, from the wedding they'd been to at Cana. He didn't look very happy, he was shaking his head at the damage done to the roof.

Jesus however was looking at the man on the mat. Smiling he said, "Son, your sins are forgiven." He looked up at the Pharisees who were sitting nearby. They seemed angry and Jesus knew that they were questioning what he had said and thinking that he had no right to forgive anyone. "Why are you thinking these things?" he asked, "Which is easier: to say to the paralytic, 'Your sins are forgiven,' or to say, 'Get up, take your mat and walk'? But so that you know the Son of Man has authority on earth to forgive sins …" Jesus looked at the man and said, "I tell you, get up, take your mat and go home."

Everyone watched in amazement as the man hesitantly stood up and picked up the mat he'd been lying on. After thanking Jesus he slowly made his way through the crowd to the door. Most of the people moved aside to let him get passed but some reached out to touch him in the hope that some of the miracle would rub off on them. The people praised Yahweh for the man's healing, saying that they had never seen anything like it before.

The man's friends ran down from the roof, not noticing the boys in their excitement. They grabbed hold of their friend and swung him around, thrilled that he could walk again. They wanted to carry him on their shoulders in a victory celebration but the man was so excited at being able to walk again he wouldn't let them.

"No," he said, "Jesus has restored my legs, let me use them!" and he ran down the street laughing. Matthew and Sam watched him from the rooftop.

Sam grinned, "Wow, he's happy!"

"I would be too! It means he no longer needs to beg for food as he will be able to work now."

"I hadn't thought of that, where I come from people who are disabled get help from the government."

Matthew shook his head, "Not here. The Romans don't help anyone except themselves. Yahweh expects us to care for our own families, but it's not always possible."

"Is that why Rachel is cooking for her brother?"

"Yes, Uncle Eli still has to care for his flock as well as look after Aunt Dinah. She has been ill for a long time so the whole family helps."

Sam realised that being ill in the first century was very different to being ill in the twenty-first. Hospitals didn't exist for one thing.

"Are there doctors here?" he asked.

"Yes, but they can be expensive and not all of them can help. That's why so many people go to Jesus. He heals everyone he sees!"

Just then the time stone began to glow and the

31

two boys were whisked away.

CHAPTER 5

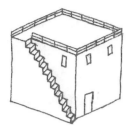

Matthew and Sam were standing next to the road at the entrance to a village. They could see Jesus and his friends approaching, talking and laughing with each other. On the opposite side of the road, a group of ten men arrived, keeping their distance from everyone else. They moved slowly and as they got closer Sam could see that most of them had deformed hands and feet and their clothes were dirty and tattered. Long strips of cloth were wrapped around their heads, covering their faces so that only their eyes could be seen. They were obviously unwell.

"What's wrong with them?" whispered Sam.

"They have leprosy," answered Matthew, "do you know of it?"

"No, at least, I've heard of it but I don't think people get it anymore, not where I come from anyway."

"It's a dreadful disease. It is highly contagious so they have to live separately from everyone else. They are not allowed in the village."

"Can their families visit them?"

"No, they can't see them either. Food is left outside the boundary wall for them to collect when there is no one else around. Lepers usually live together in groups so that they can help each other but it is very hard for them."

"What has happened to their hands and feet?"

"The disease causes them to lose all feeling so it is easy to damage them when they can't feel pain. If they get very bad they have to have their fingers and toes cut off."

Sam shuddered, he was really glad he lived in a time when doctors and medicine were readily available. As Jesus got closer one of the men stood out from the group and called out in a loud voice,

"Jesus, Master, have pity on us!"

Sam glanced at Matthew curiously then turned his attention back to Jesus to see what he would do. Jesus stopped and looked at the men.

"Go, show yourselves to the priests," he said. The

men turned slowly and limped off towards the village. As they did so they began to straighten up and walk more confidently. By the time they got to the other side of the low wall that indicated the village boundary, the men were walking normally, just like anyone else. One man turned around and ran back to Jesus, loudly praising God. He fell at Jesus' feet and thanked him for healing him of leprosy.

Jesus looked around at those standing near him and asked, "Were not all ten cleansed? Where are the other nine? Was there no-one else to give praise to God except this foreigner?" Then, speaking to the man at his feet he said, "Get up and go, your faith has made you well." The man stood up and still rejoicing, went into the village to the synagogue to find the priest. Jesus and his friends followed at a more sedate pace.

Sam was about to ask Matthew about the man being a foreigner and why they needed to see the priest when the stone began to hum.

Back in Bethlehem Rachel was still busy preparing a meal for Eli and Dinah when the two boys raced in excitedly.

"Ima! We've just seen Jesus heal a lame man and

ten lepers!"

"They lowered him through the roof! Rachel, why did the lepers have to see the priest? And why did Jesus call him a foreigner?"

"Boys, slow down!" Rachel laughed, "I take it you've been travelling again? Sit down and tell me, but slowly, one at a time!" The boys sat at the table and described what had happened while Rachel carried on preparing vegetables.

"Those men must have been determined to see Jesus if they dug through the roof," she said.

"It was the only way they could get in, the house was so crowded!" Matthew said, helping himself to some sliced carrots and passing some to Sam.

"No more or there won't be enough for dinner!" Rachel scraped the last of the chopped vegetables into the cooking pot. "I wonder whose house it was. They can't have been too happy about the damage, they would have had to repair it before nightfall!"

"We saw Peter, he was shaking his head and looking cross. Perhaps it was his house?" Sam looked at Matthew who nodded in agreement. "I don't suppose he was too cross though," Sam went on, "not when the man got up and walked away!"

"No, the whole place was in an uproar, everyone

was laughing and praising Yahweh!"

"Well, everyone except the Pharisees. Why can't they be happy for people for a change?" asked Sam.

They reminded him of one of his teachers at school. Last winter his class had wanted to organise a snowball fight and a snowman building competition with the rest of their year. Everyone was looking forward to it until this one teacher had spoilt it with a load of rules. They'd given up in the end, it was too much trouble. Thinking about rules reminded Sam of his questions.

"Why did Jesus tell the lepers to see the priests?" he asked.

"Because it is written in the law that Yahweh gave to Moses in the desert," answered Rachel. "They have to examine the person afflicted by the disease to make sure it has all gone. If the priest says they are cured the one who was sick is allowed back into the community. It is important to keep the rest of the village safe."

"I guess there are some rules that we shouldn't break," said Sam.

"Definitely, especially Yahweh's!" said Rachel.

"And Ima's!" laughed Matthew.

"Oh, most definitely mine!" agreed Rachel as she and Sam joined in the laughter.

◆ ◆ ◆

Later that afternoon, Sam was sat alone under the fig tree. Rachel was resting in the house, her chores finally completed and Matthew had gone to his room to collect a board game. He had promised to teach Sam how to play a game that sounded very much like draughts. He took the time stone out of his pouch to look at the symbols. As he did so it began to hum and in a flash of blue light, Sam was once again on a hill with the sheep. He grinned, he could see young Rachel in the distance. He was guessing that the stone had brought him back to collect her before taking them further back in time.

CHAPTER 6

Rachel was sitting on the grass, watching the sheep while she plaited a rope of goat hair. Approaching from behind, Sam called out to her and she immediately jumped up and ran to greet him. Their last adventure with the Israelites in the wilderness had made them firm friends.

"Sam! I was just thinking about you," she said linking arms with him and pulling him down to sit on the grass. Sam laughed,

"Are you still dreaming about eating manna?"

"No, but it was good wasn't it!"

"Have I been away long?" asked Sam. Last time, the stone had brought him back the day after he had left, although when he was at home, he had waited over a week before travelling again.

"No, only two days. My cousins are going back

to Jerusalem soon so I may not be here every day. The town is a lot quieter now that people are going home after the census."

"Will you miss the sheep?"

"Yes, but I will be busy helping Ima and I shall still come to bring food for my brothers. I am allowed to stay sometimes too."

Sam smiled, he hoped the stone would keep bringing him to the hillside, he liked listening to the soft sounds of the sheep as they wandered about.

The hum of the time stone mingled with the bleating of the lambs. Holding on to the stone, the two friends prepared themselves for their next adventure.

"Jerusalem!" declared Rachel, "Look, there's the temple. Isn't it wonderful!" Rachel stared in awe at the temple built by King Solomon. They had arrived in the time before the temple had been destroyed by King Nebuchadnezzar and the Babylonians and it looked magnificent.

"I wonder which King is in power?" she said.

"How can we find out? We can't just go up to someone and ask!"

"No, and we would be safer if we kept ourselves hidden. Not all the kings followed Yahweh and some were particularly bad!"

"Perhaps we could go inside?"

"Ohhh yes, let's!" said Rachel, excited at seeing the inside of the famous building, "but we can only go into the outer court."

"Why?"

"Because you are a Gentile. That's right, isn't it? You are not Hebrew?"

"No, I'm English. What's a Gentile?"

"Anyone who isn't a Hebrew. What is English?"

"Someone from England. It's a country thousands of miles away in the north. It's a lot colder and wetter."

"Oh, well anyone is allowed into the outer court but only Hebrews can go beyond it. Even I can only go into the next one. It's called the court of women because we are not allowed any further."

Rachel and Sam made their way up the temple steps and entered the outer court. There were a lot of people inside so it was easy to hide among the crowd. They tried to listen in on conversations to get an idea of whose reign they had arrived at but the noise of people and animals was horrendous making it hard to hear. Near to the entrance of the women's court were tables set up where people seemed to be doing business.

"What are they doing?" asked Sam.

"People need to exchange their goods to buy an animal for sacrifice. The Levites work out how much their goods are worth then give them a receipt for their value. The people exchange the receipt for an animal that is worth the same. The animals are over there, look." Sam looked to where Rachel was pointing and saw cages filled with birds and stalls full of sheep and cattle.

"But they're lambs, just like the one we rescued!"

"Yes, some of the lambs my brothers raise are used for temple sacrifices. They take them to Jerusalem every year."

Sam looked at Rachel aghast. He remembered Rachel explaining the need for sacrifice when they went back in time to see David. He hadn't realised it was such big business though.

"How many courts are there?" he asked, trying to change the subject to something more acceptable.

"Well, past the court of women is the men's court and after that the court of the priests. Then there is the Holy Place with the Holy of Holies at the back, behind the curtain."

"So who is allowed in there?"

"Only the priests on duty for that day can enter the Holy Place. The Holy of Holies is forbidden to everyone except the High Priest and he is only allowed in once a year."

"So what would happen if he went in at the wrong time?"

"He would die."

Sam gulped, in their last adventure together, Yahweh had been hidden in a cloud that flashed with lightning and had been powerful enough to make a path through the sea then destroy a whole army of Egyptians. Now Rachel was telling him that he would kill anyone who went into the wrong room at the wrong time! Sam decided he wasn't going anywhere unless Rachel went with him!

While they had been looking around, the Levites had packed up for the day and the court had got quieter as people went back to their homes. The children went over to the animal pens and hid themselves behind a stone pillar. They had no idea why the time stone had brought them there but it seemed to be the right thing for them to do.

They had just got settled when there was a commotion near the entrance. A group of guards accompanied a tall, good looking man dressed in rich robes and the few remaining people in the court immediately stopped talking and bowed. Various greetings rang out around the court.

"Your Majesty!"

"Hail to the King!"

"Hail Uzziah, King of Judah!"

Rachel gasped as she realised when in time they were. She also had a good idea of what would happen next.

"So is he a good king or a bad one?" asked Sam.

"Well, if my timing is right he was a good king right up until today!"

"So what made him bad?"

"He went into the Holy Place and burnt incense on the altar."

"Why would he? That's crazy!" Sam squeaked, he wasn't looking forward to this at all.

"At first he was faithful and always followed Yahweh's laws so Yahweh had blessed him, making him extremely rich and powerful. He became famous throughout many nations but he forgot that it was Yahweh who had made it all possible.

King Uzziah became proud and believed he could do whatever he wanted. Eighty priests were brave enough to follow him into the Holy Place so that they could confront him."

Sam listened, eyes wide and mouth agape.

"What happened?" he whispered.

"Watch, he'll be coming out soon."

Suddenly, they heard the sound of people hurrying through the inner court. As they watched, priests and guards stumbled past in their haste to leave the temple. In the midst of them, a tall man tried desperately to keep up with them. Head bowed, King Uzziah was no longer the handsome man that had entered the sanctuary. As Sam stared at the once-proud king, he could see that he looked just like the ten men who had stood on the road waiting for Jesus. Yahweh hadn't killed the king, he had given him leprosy!

CHAPTER 7

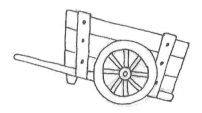

Sam gaped at Rachel as they stood in the street of a large village. The stone had moved them from the temple in Jerusalem to a different location but Sam's head was still full of King Uzziah covered in leprosy.

"So did he get better or did he die?" he asked.

"He lived for another eleven years but was never cured. His son took over as king because Uzziah had to live in isolation from everyone."

Sam's head was spinning. He really couldn't get used to the idea that Yahweh would heal one person but harm another.

"I don't understand either," admitted Rachel, "Maybe when you go home again you can ask your rabbi then come back and explain to me!"

Sam sighed, "That sounds like a good idea," he

said.

The rumbling sound of wooden wheels on the stony ground gradually got louder as a small procession of donkeys pulling carts approached the street where they were standing. They were led by a soldier who drove a chariot pulled by two smart horses. He looked like he was more used to commanding a large army than a few carts filled with goods. Unfortunately for him, he was also afflicted with leprosy.

"Not another one!" groaned Sam.

"He's stopped outside that house," said Rachel, "Let's get closer."

The children crossed the street so that it wouldn't be too obvious they were watching the events on the other side. A messenger came out and spoke to the soldier.

"Elisha says you are to wash in the River Jordan seven times. Then you will be clean and your flesh restored," he said.

The soldier was furious, "Could he not come out himself and speak the name of his God over me?" he said, "The rivers of Damascus are better than any in Israel, why could I not wash in those and be cleansed?" Turning his chariot, the soldier angrily shook the reins in his hands and yelled a command. The horses galloped off almost causing the chariot to overturn. At the end of the street, the soldier pulled the horses to a halt, giving time for his servants to catch up with him. Rachel and Sam raced after the servants to hear what they would say.

"Master, if the prophet had told you to do something amazing or difficult, would you not have done it? Surely it is more worthy for you to do this simple task?"

The soldier realised that his servant was right and taking a deep breath he calmed down. He drove his chariot slowly to the river then climbed down. The children followed on behind with his servants. At the water's edge, the servants helped the soldier remove his outer garments and he stepped into the river. Sinking beneath the surface so that the water covered his head the soldier came up again, shivering. He did this six times but each time he came up his skin was the same. The soldier turned to look at the servant who had encouraged him to do as Elisha had said.

"Once more Master, the prophet said you must do this seven times," the servant pleaded with his master who he loved like a father, "Please, sire."

The soldier sighed and sank once more beneath the water. When he came up again he shook his head, spraying water everywhere. Rachel, Sam and the servants gasped when they saw the soldier looking young and healthy with no sign of leprosy anywhere! Laughing, the soldier climbed out of the river and got dressed. Driving his chariot back to the prophet's house, he praised the God of Elisha while his servants and the children followed behind, cheering. When they arrived, Elisha was standing at the door waiting. The soldier climbed down and spoke,

"Now I know that there is no God in all the world except in Israel. Please now accept a gift from your servant."

"As surely as the Lord lives, whom I serve, I will not accept a thing," answered Elisha. The soldier tried to persuade him to accept his gifts but Elisha stood firm. Eventually, the soldier promised to honour Yahweh and worship no other god but him for the rest of his life. The prophet blessed him and the soldier returned to his chariot.

As the servants turned the carts around to begin their journey home the time stone hummed, glowed and whisked the children away. They arrived back at the hillside in Bethlehem. Sam sat down and hugged his knees.

"So who was the soldier?" he asked.

"His name was Naaman and he came from Aram. He learnt about Elisha from a Hebrew servant girl and because his king valued him highly, he allowed Naaman to go and see him."

"I wonder why he had to wash in the river? It's not like you can wash leprosy off is it?"

"No, you can't. I think sometimes we have to do something that shows how strong our faith is. If he'd given up after six times he wouldn't have been healed. It was important for him to persevere to show that he trusted Yahweh to heal him."

Sam laughed, "His servant was right, wasn't he? Naaman would have agreed straight away if he'd been asked to do something difficult!"

"Yes but sometimes the answer is really simple. There is more to the story though."

"Oh? Why what happened?"

"Elisha's servant was greedy and ran after him to ask for money. He told Naaman a lie about two young men asking for help. He said Elisha had sent him to ask for silver and clothes."

"So did Naaman give them to him?"

"Oh yes, he believed the story and he was

pleased to help but Elisha found out."

"I'm thinking that this didn't end well," sighed Sam, shaking his head.

"It didn't. The servant, whose name was Gehazi, got leprosy and had to leave."

Sam groaned, he wasn't at all sure he wanted to hear anymore. He was very grateful that scientists and doctors had learnt how to cure a lot of the problems that people had suffered from in ancient times. Even so, he thought, there are still a lot of things that haven't been cured. Maybe we should all start listening to God a bit more. Rachel glanced over at Sam, she knew he was struggling with the things he had seen and heard.

"Maybe you need to go home and speak to your rabbi," she said.

"Yeah, I need to speak to someone who knows Yahweh but who understands my time as well."

"Just as long as you come back and tell me what he says!" said Rachel, jumping up from the grass, "Bye Sam, see you tomorrow?"

"Hope so," Sam grinned and as Rachel ran off back to the shepherds' camp, the time stone glowed and took Sam home.

CHAPTER 8

The rest of that week passed by in a blur. Sam did his chores, went to school, worked on his science project and did everything he usually did. He handed his homework in on time and hung around with Alex during break. Ollie and Jack still waited outside the school gates to annoy him, though thankfully not as often as they used to. Nothing had changed, so why did Sam feel unsettled? He suspected it had a lot to do with his time travel adventures but unfortunately there was no one in the present time that he could talk to. He looked forward to Friday when the youth group met at the local church. Maybe Chris, one of the leaders, would be able to help.

For once, Sam wasn't bothered about beating Alex at air hockey and his lack of expertise at the Jenga tower had it crashing down before they'd even started.

"Sam, what's wrong with you?" complained Ben, as bent down to pick up and re-stack the fallen blocks.

"Yeah," agreed Alex, "You've been a grouch all week."

"Sorry," sighed Sam, "I think maybe I need to talk to Chris. I'll see you later." Sam slouched off, hands in his pockets, watched by his three friends.

"What's going on?" asked Jamie, looking at Alex with a puzzled frown.

"No idea, but he's been miserable all week. I know he gets bullied sometimes, but I thought he was dealing with that."

"Oh, that's tough. Chris will sort it, he's one of the good guys," Jamie said, turning back to the tower which was back in its upright state, "Go on Ben, you first."

Sam found Chris trying to fix the table football which had jammed after some over-enthusiastic play.

"There, that should do it," he said, "try being a bit less aggressive, it's getting old, like me!"

The boys around the table laughed and resumed their game, cheering loudly whenever a goal was scored. Sam raised his eyebrows and looked at Chris.

"Not sure that's going to happen," he said.

Chris laughed, "No, but it's worth a try. How're you doing Sam?" Sam considered the question, still not sure about what he was going to say.

"Can I talk to you about something?"

"Sure, let's sit over there in the corner. It's out of the way so we won't be overheard."

Sam breathed a sigh of relief. He didn't want anyone else getting in on this, it was hard enough as it was. He felt the same as when they'd visited Daniel and told him about the time stone. Not that he was going to say anything to Chris about that. Not unless he had to anyway.

"So, how can I help," asked Chris once they were settled.

"Erm, well," Sam pulled a face not knowing where to start. Chris waited patiently, giving Sam time to collect his thoughts. "It's just, I don't understand why God heals some people but then makes other people sick."

"Oh, that's a good question and you're not the first person to ask it. But do you think God does make people sick?"

Sam thought about King Uzziah and Elisha's servant, Gehazi.

"Yes, definitely," he said.

Chris raised his eyebrows, "May I ask why?" he asked. He'd had this conversation many times but no one had ever been as definite as Sam about God's involvement.

"Well, I know about King Uzziah and Elisha's servant getting leprosy and I know they probably deserved it. But Jesus told the man on the mat his sins were forgiven so why didn't God forgive Uzziah? He'd been good up till then!"

Chris nodded, wondering if there was something specific that had sparked off Sam's concerns.

"Is there someone close to you who is sick Sam?"

"Noo," Sam groaned, how could he explain without telling Chris about the stone? Then he remembered Eli's wife, "Not close, a friend's aunt."

"Would it help to bring your friend to group?"

Sam shook his head, "He doesn't live here, I met him when I was on holiday in Norfolk." At least that was true, even if there was a lot more to it!

Chris paused and prayed silently, asking God for wisdom.

"A lot of stuff that happened in the Old Testament happened because people refused to listen to God and obey his laws," he said, "Some of those laws were designed to keep them healthy. They didn't have the benefit of all the things we have today, like modern medicine and fridges to stop food going off. Eating the wrong things could easily have made them ill."

"Like eating too much junk food today," said Sam.

"Exactly."

"But those weren't the laws that Uzziah broke."

"No, Uzziah broke laws of honour. God is righteous and holy, which means he is totally sinless. He has never thought, said or done anything wrong ever. Some laws are designed to help us be like him."

"But that's impossible!" said Sam, thinking about all the times he'd thought things he really hoped no one would ever know about.

"Yes, it is, which is why God gives us lots of second chances to try to get it right. King Uzziah knew that what he did was wrong but he was proud. He wanted to prove he was just as powerful as God. God showed him that he wasn't."

"But what if he'd said sorry?"

"He did eventually and God forgave him but he still had to suffer the consequences of his actions."

"What do you mean?"

"Well, leprosy can be cured now but in those days they only knew how to stop it from spreading. If God had healed Uzziah he would eventually get so wrapped up in his rich life again that he would forget what God had done for him. Keeping the leprosy until the day he died was a constant reminder to him that God was all-powerful and not someone to be taken lightly. I'm sure he was a much nicer person when he died than when he first went into the temple and broke God's law."

That reminded Sam of the Israelites during their trek through the desert. Even after all the miracles of crossing the Red Sea and eating food from heaven they still took it all for granted and forgot about Yahweh.

"So, why did Jesus forgive the lame man?"

Chris smiled, "Jesus' whole purpose was to forgive. God desperately wants us, his children, to have a relationship with him. He wants us to get to know him, to be friends with him. Jesus came to teach us the best way to live but more importantly, he came to make a way for us to be forgiven forever without the need for repeated sacrifices."

"Rachel said that's why they sacrificed the lambs at the temple," said Sam, forgetting that he wasn't supposed to talk about her. Chris looked at him curiously, Sam seemed to know a lot about the Jewish faith.

"Is she Jewish, your friend?"

"Er, I guess so, she's from Israel," answered Sam, biting his lip as he realised his mistake.

"Well, she's quite right, the Jews sacrifice the lamb to atone for their sins. That means they offer it to God as a way of saying sorry. Christians believe that Jesus came to be like those lambs so that we will always be forgiven whenever we truly repent."

Sam looked up, horrified, "Is that why he died?"

"Yes, it is. Now we can all be friends of God because Jesus made the ultimate sacrifice. He was our substitute, he gave his life in exchange for ours so God no longer needs us to sacrifice animals." Chris smiled kindly, "Has that helped with your dilemma?"

"I'm not sure," answered Sam honestly, "I think I

may have a lot more to learn."

"That's okay, Sam. It's much better to take your time so that you understand just who God is and what he has done for us. Always remember though that he loves you very much."

"Thank you, you're not the first to tell me that."

"Well, I'm glad you have some good friends, Sam. I'm here for you too, if you need to ask anything else."

Sam smiled, "Thanks, you'll probably wish you hadn't said that!"

Chris laughed, "Anytime, Sam, I've enjoyed talking to you!"

Walking home that night, Sam felt a lot better than he had at the beginning of the week. Chris may not have answered all his questions but he had certainly helped him to understand a bit more. Now he needed to go back to see Rachel and tell her what he had learned. Thank goodness Chris hadn't asked anything else about her! Then Sam realised that he needed to be careful what he said to Rachel too so that he didn't talk about things she knew nothing about. Young Rachel only knew about the baby Jesus that the angels had called Messiah. She wouldn't know about Jesus as a grown-up until she had grown up herself. Even then, she would only know about some of Jesus' miracles. She didn't know he was going to die a horrible death. Time travel was definitely more complicated than he had first thought!

CHAPTER 9

Over the next few days, Sam thought about what Chris had said. He understood that God was trying to teach them to be better people but he was still struggling with the scary God he had seen at work on his travels back in time. One afternoon, as he was leaving school with his head well and truly stuck in ancient Israel, Sam didn't notice Ollie waiting at the gate.

"Well if it isn't the little sparrow, all on his lonesome!" taunted Ollie who was leaning on the fence with his arms folded. Sam looked up, searching for Jack who was usually nearby, joining in with whatever Ollie had to say. The two were inseparable, so where was he? Unseen by Sam, Jack had crept up behind him and with a firm shove, he pushed Sam to the ground. Jack grabbed Sam's rucksack and ran off, closely followed by Ollie. As they ran, the two bullies opened up the bag and after tipping the contents onto the ground, threw it over the fence. Other kids walked past not wanting to get involved, all except Kate, who started to collect up Sam's stuff.

"Thanks," said Sam who had picked himself up and joined Kate in gathering up his belongings.

"You should stand up to them," she said, "Where's your rucksack?"

"They threw it over the fence."

Kate looked at Sam and sighed.

"Come on," she said, "Let's pack your stuff and I'll walk home with you."

"I thought you lived near the park. That's in the opposite direction."

"I do, but I'm meeting my sister at her friend's place, they've been on study leave for GCSE's but they're back in school tomorrow. She lives around the corner from you."

"How come you know so much?" asked Sam. Kate grinned,

"I asked. I'm curious about people I like."

"Oh," Sam blushed, "So erm, who's your sister?"

Kate was very outspoken, unlike anyone else he knew.

"Dayle. With a Y," grinned Kate. Sam looked up, surprised.

"But she's nothing like you!" he exclaimed, comparing calm Dayle with exuberant Kate. Plus Kate did have very red hair, unlike Dayle who was blonde.

"No, I'm adopted."

"I, um, I didn't know," Sam stammered, embarrassed.

"Oh, that's okay. I was adopted as a baby so I've never known any other family. Dad jokes about them finding me in the strawberry patch but I don't mind. I know they chose me and love me just as much as their other kids."

"So, who else is there then?"

"Just Logan, he's in sixth form. He wants to be a doctor so he's always studying. He's hoping to go to London for uni. I want to act or dance or both!" she said, suddenly running ahead and spinning around.

Sam laughed, he reckoned that whatever she did, it would be loud and energetic!

"That's better, I like it when you laugh. You've been grumpy this week," Kate said, smiling.

"Sorry, I didn't think anyone would notice."

"We've all noticed. Dayle asked me to ask Alex what was wrong but he didn't know."

Sam shrugged. He liked that his new friends cared about him but he had no idea how to explain why he'd been so miserable.

"It's not Ollie and Jack," he said, keen to show that they at least weren't the cause of his misery.

"So what is it then?" persisted Kate. Realising that she wasn't going to let this go, Sam took a deep breath and with words coming out in a rush said,

"I think God is really real but I don't think he's like the kind old man with a beard we think of at Christmas. I think sometimes he gets cross and is very scary."

"Oh," Kate paused, "Have you done something wrong?"

"No! At least, no more than anyone else has. It's just that, well, he frightens me."

Kate looked at Sam curiously. "You sound as though you've actually met him!"

Sam sighed, "I've seen him," he said. Kate stopped in the middle of the pavement and turned to face Sam, eyes wide in surprise.

"Wow! Seriously? When?"

Good question thought Sam. Was it only last week or was it thousands of years ago, when the stone took him back in time to the exodus? How could he explain without telling Kate his secret? Coming to a decision, Sam took a deep breath and asked,

"Do you have time to come to my house?"

"Sure, I can phone Dayle and say I'll be a bit late, she won't mind."

Sam planned to show Kate the stone and explain the meaning of the symbols. Then he'd tell her about joining the exodus and seeing God in the cloud. The stone, however, had other ideas. No sooner had Sam picked it up off his bedside table when it began to hum.

"Oh no," he thought, not knowing what to do. In a panic he grabbed hold of Kate, this wasn't in the plan!

CHAPTER 10

Sam let go of Kate and covered his ears. Kate's screams were loud enough to bring the rest of the neighbourhood into the courtyard! They had arrived back in Bethlehem under the fig tree in Rachel's garden. Kate was practically hysterical. Finally drawing breath, she stopped screaming and gasped,

"Where are we? And where's my uniform?" She looked at Sam, "Why are you wearing a dress?"

Sam calmly placed the stone into its pouch and looked up to see Matthew and Rachel running out of the house. When they saw Kate they both burst out laughing.

"First time?" asked Matthew.

"Oh, my dear, don't fret," said Rachel, "You'll get used to it!" Kate looked in horror at the two strangers in front of her. Then she looked at Sam who appeared far happier and more relaxed than she'd seen him all week. Sam grinned,

"Rachel, Matthew, this is Kate. She's a friend from home." Rachel immediately wrapped Kate in a hug.

"Welcome to Bethlehem, Kate," she said.

"Bethlehem?" squeaked Kate, looking at Sam in astonishment.

"Yeah," he replied, "Sometime in the first century, in Jesus' time." Kate's eyes nearly popped out of her head.

"Come, sit," said Rachel to Kate, "You'll soon feel better, the dizziness doesn't last long."

"I think you need to explain to your friend, Sam," grinned Matthew, sitting down underneath the tree. So, taking a deep breath and with help from Rachel and Matthew, Sam told Kate the story of the time stone. When he got to the part where he and Rachel had joined the exodus and saw Yahweh in the cloud with the lightning, Kate let out a gasp.

"No wonder you were frightened!" she said. Sam nodded,

"There's a lot more, I've been here a few times now, but I spoke to Chris and he helped a bit. He's our rabbi," he explained to Rachel and Matthew.

"Does Chris know about the stone?" asked Kate.

"No, no one at home knows, only you." Sam looked at Rachel, "The last time I was here, you were preparing a meal for Eli and Dinah. How is she, is she better?"

"Oh, Sam, I haven't taken it yet! It's still the same day!" laughed Rachel.

Sam shook his head, "It's been over a week at home!" he said.

"I'd only just got my game from my room," laughed Matthew, "then I heard screaming. I thought someone was being attacked!" Kate's face turned the colour of her hair.

"Sorry," she said, "It was a bit of a shock!"

"Oh, don't I know it! The first time I travelled I was shaking like a leaf!" said Rachel.

"You didn't scream though," joined in Sam. Kate nudged him with her elbow,

"I'm sure you wondered what was going on the first time you arrived!"

They all laughed as they each remembered their first experience of travelling through time.

"How would you all like to come with me to deliver this food?" asked Rachel, "You will be able to see some more of the town." Sam and Kate agreed and while Rachel went to sort out the meal, Matthew introduced Kate to the goat.

"Does she have a name?" asked Kate as she scratched the goat's ears.

"Hepzibah," said Matthew, "It means 'my delight is in her.' She gives us lots of milk so she is living up to her name."

Kate laughed, "My name means innocent," she said, "I'm afraid I don't always live up to mine!" The boys joined in with her laughter, each of them thinking of times when they had not been so innocent either.

"Do you think that's why Yahweh gets cross with us?" asked Sam.

"What do you mean?" frowned Matthew.

"Sam is afraid of Yahweh because he thinks he's always angry," said Kate.

"Is he though? I know he gets angry when we break his laws but he always forgives us. Ima was angry with me when I didn't shut the gate properly once. Hepzibah got out and ate the basket of fruit a neighbour was taking to market. I had to work for him for a week to repay the debt. She didn't stay angry though, I know that Ima loves me and she forgave me straight away, well, almost."

Sam grinned, "I'm sure you remember to shut the gate now!"

"Always! I have learned that lesson for sure!"

At that point, Rachel came out carrying a large cooking pot wrapped in a cloth to keep the food warm.

"Matthew, please would you get the basket that is on the table? There's some bread and wine in it for them." Rachel looked at Sam and Kate, "I think we should introduce you as friends from Jericho."

"Why Jericho?" asked Kate.

"That's where I first met Matthew. I was stood under the tree where Jesus called Zaccheus," answered Sam.

"We were visiting my sister who was sick," said Rachel, "I had been expecting to see Sam again, I just didn't know when."

"Does this mean I tell you then, while you're still young?"

"Yes, but not yet. I will let you know when the time is right."

Kate was understandably confused by this conversation but before she could say anything, Matthew came back with the basket.

The visit to see Eli and Dinah left Sam feeling sad. He could see that Matthew's aunt was very sick and she didn't look as though she was going to get better. Eli was grateful for the food and thanked Rachel for all the help she was giving to them.

"Why doesn't Yahweh heal her?" asked Sam when they got back.

"I don't know, Sam," replied Rachel, "But we must still praise him and trust him to do what is right, just as David wrote in his psalms."

"It's not fair!" said Sam.

"No. Sometimes life isn't fair but Yahweh never said it would be," she said taking the now-empty basket into the house. Matthew, Sam and Kate were still outside when the stone began to hum.

"Ready for another trip?" grinned Sam to Kate.

CHAPTER 11

The three friends were stood on the outside of a large crowd of people. They tried pushing their way through to see what was happening at the front but the crowd held them back.

"I suppose Jesus is in the middle of it all," said Sam.

"Probably," agreed Matthew, "They do seem to follow him everywhere."

"So, where exactly are we?" asked Kate. The two boys sniffed the air.

"Don't know, I can't smell fish so it's not Galilee," grinned Sam. Kate raised her eyebrows.

"Fish?"

"Galilee is a very fishy place!" Matthew laughed, "I don't suppose it matters where we are, only that

Jesus is here."

"Yes, I just wish I could hear what he was saying," said Sam.

Just then they heard Jesus' disciples speaking to some of the women, telling them to hold on to their children and keep them away from Jesus. One woman, standing in front of Sam, spoke up.

"We just want him to bless our children," she said. Jesus raised his voice in response.

"Let the little children come to me, and do not hinder them, for the kingdom of heaven belongs to such as these."

The crowd parted and allowed the woman through with her child, closely followed by Sam, Kate and Matthew. Other women stood with her, holding up their little ones, as Jesus prayed for each one. Satisfied, the women left, leaving the three friends standing at the front of the crowd. Jesus looked over at them and smiled.

"Matthew!" he said, "You are a long way from home. How is your Ima?"

"She is well thank you, but aunt Dinah is sick." Matthew looked down at the ground in an attempt to hide his fears. No-one expected her to live much longer. Concerned for his friend, Sam plucked up his courage and spoke out.

"We were hoping you would come and heal her," he said. Jesus looked closely at Sam and smiled. Sam squirmed, he felt that Jesus could see right inside him and knew every thought he had ever had. He made Sam feel that there was nothing that Jesus didn't know about him and Sam wasn't sure that was such a good thing!

Jesus laughed, "Don't be afraid little sparrow! You are well-loved by my father!" He turned to Matthew and put his hand on his shoulder, "I am travelling to Jerusalem for Passover. I will come on the way." Matthew thanked him and the three moved away from the crowd. With their mission completed, the stone hummed and in a flash of blue light, it took them back to Bethlehem.

After finishing their meal the three children told Rachel about their encounter with Jesus. Kate didn't say much, which was unusual for her, but Sam didn't notice she was quiet as he still couldn't get over how he had felt when Jesus had looked at him.

"It was as if he really did know who I was," he said, "But how could he? I don't even belong in this time!"

Rachel smiled, "Many people believe that he is the Messiah. Perhaps Yahweh whispered your name to him!"

"Don't you remember the story about how Yahweh even cares for the smallest sparrow?" asked Matthew, "He could probably see you were frightened and just wanted to make you feel better."

"Yes, you're probably right. It's good that he said he would come though, isn't it?"

They all agreed and wondered how long it would take for Jesus to get to Bethlehem. Not knowing where he was when they met him they were unable to say how far he needed to travel.

"And he'll probably visit other places on the way!" said Rachel as she tidied the house before sending them off to bed.

With Simon out in the fields looking after the sheep and Adah visiting her mother, Kate had their room to herself. As she settled down to sleep she thought about all that had happened since walking home with Sam. She hadn't liked to say anything in front of Rachel and Matthew but she understood how Sam had felt. Jesus had looked at her the same way and she was quite certain she had heard him say her name too.

◆ ◆ ◆

The next morning after breakfast they all agreed that they should go to see Eli and Dinah to prepare them for Jesus' visit. Rachel packed up another basket of food and they set off across the town.

As they approached the house, they could hear laughter and singing. Hurrying inside they were amazed to see Dinah sweeping the floor. She looked better than ever, even from the time before she got sick!

"Rachel, welcome," she said, "Isn't it wonderful, I am completely well!"

Immediately, Rachel put down her basket and enveloped Dinah in a big hug.

"How did this happen?" she asked. Just then, Eli came into the room and spoke to the children.

"Jesus came last night!" he said, "He told us you had asked him to come. How can we ever thank you?" Eli explained that Jesus had arrived quite late with two of his friends and they had prayed for Dinah. As soon as they had finished, she had opened her eyes, got up and offered them the bread and wine that Rachel had brought earlier. They left soon after before news of his visit got out and drew the crowds.

"He seemed a little sad," said Dinah, "I think he was tired. It must be exhausting being surrounded by all those people all the time!"

The rest of the day was spent celebrating Dinah's return to good health, praising Yahweh for his goodness and catching up on all the news that Dinah had missed while she was sick. As she had been ill for a long time, she and Rachel had a lot of talking to do.

Matthew, Sam and Kate wandered out into the garden.

"Thank you for asking him," said Matthew.

Sam shrugged, "I didn't know what else to do. I reckoned the stone must have brought us back for a reason and maybe that was it."

"So what happens now?" asked Kate.

"Dunno. Whenever we've done what the stone brought me for it takes me home again."

"Perhaps we should go back to my home," said Matthew, "I'll just go and tell Ima we're leaving." He ran into the house just as the time stone started to hum.

CHAPTER 12

Sitting on the bed in Sam's room, Kate shook her head to clear the dizzy feeling they all experienced with travelling through time.

"Did that actually happen?" she said, looking at Sam incredulously. She couldn't decide whether she had just travelled through time with a flashing blue stone or whether Sam had simply hit her over the head with it.

"It happened," grinned Sam, "Awesome isn't it!"

"I've just met Jesus!" Kate exclaimed, then her face paled, "Sam, he spoke to me too. He said my name."

"Then he does know who we are," Sam paused, "And where we're from! Kate, you mustn't tell anyone. Please, it has to be our secret!" Kate nodded, who would believe them anyway!

Sam felt a lot happier now that he had someone he could talk to without having to think about how to explain himself. That Friday, at youth group, he annihilated Alex at air hockey, winning with a clear ten points.

"Well, you've certainly changed since last week!" said Alex, throwing down the puck in disgust at finally relinquishing his championship. He clapped Sam on the back to show there were no hard feelings, pleased to see Sam in a better mood.

During the break before the God Slot, Sam went to find Chris.

"Hi Sam, need to talk?"

"Yes please, you said I could?" Sam hoped that Chris had meant what he had said the week before.

"Of course. How's your friend's aunt?"

Sam grinned, "Better! Jesus healed her!"

"Wow, that's fantastic. I'm pleased for your friend and especially pleased that you're so sure it was Jesus who healed her."

Sam nodded, that was one thing he did know about. Seeing Jesus perform his miracles meant that Sam was able to say for certain that Jesus had done those things written about in the bible. But who was he? Rachel said he was the Messiah but what did that mean?

"I do believe that," said Sam, "But I'm not really sure who he is. My friend called him the Messiah but I don't know what that means."

"Is this your Jewish friend?"

"Mmm, yes," Sam pulled a face, he must remember to watch what he was saying!

"That's okay, Sam. The Jews believe that the Messiah is someone who will be sent by God to save them and their nation. Some think he will be a political leader and fight for them. Others think he will solve the problems of hunger and poverty. Then there are a few who believe he has already come in the form of Jesus."

"But he's just a man, isn't he? And what about the rest of us, won't he save us too?"

Chris smiled, "Well, Christians believe that Jesus is the Son of God. If you read the story of his birth in Luke's gospel, you will see that although Mary was his mother, his father was God himself. That means that yes, he was a man but he was also God at the same time." Sam looked at Chris doubtfully.

"Right," he said, chewing on his bottom lip as he

tried to get his head around Chris' words.

Chris laughed, "It's okay Sam, it sounds impossible but that's what it says. A lot of people struggle to understand it. Sometimes we just have to accept what the bible tells us, it's what we call having faith. Faith means believing in things that don't always make sense to us but somehow we just know they are true."

Sam nodded, he of all people should know that! Travelling through time and seeing things that happened centuries ago was definitely impossible, but he'd done it loads of times. Then he remembered what Jesus had said when Sam had asked him to heal Dinah.

"You are well-loved by my father!"

Sam shivered, it was almost as if he could hear Jesus saying it to him now. If Jesus' father was God then that meant that God loved Sam. He looked at Chris who seemed so sure about what he believed. Sam still had a lot of questions but he was beginning to understand a lot more too. Perhaps the next time he went to Israel he would get a better idea of who Jesus was.

Sam thanked Chris and went back to his friends. He looked over at Kate who was chatting to her sister Dayle. He grinned at how different the two girls were and wondered what Dayle would say if she knew about Kate's adventure. Kate looked up and grinned back, at least Sam had someone he could talk to now. Someone who shared his secret, someone else who understood the secret of the time stone!

GLOSSARY

Abba - *Dad, daddy*

Atone - *Make amends*

Census - *Official count of the population*

Chariot - *Small, light, 2-wheeled open carriage*

Exodus - *Israelites' escape from Egypt*

Gentile - *Anyone who isn't a Hebrew*

Ima - *Mum, mummy*

Incense - *Spice burnt for its sweet smell*

Levites - *Assistants to the priests in the temple.*

Messiah - *Saviour of the world*

Ornate - *Decorative*

Passover - *Celebration to remember the Exodus*

Persevere - *Keep trying*

Portico - *A porch, its roof held up by columns*

Repent - *Being really sorry*

Saba - *Grandfather*

Sacrifice - *Giving up something valuable*

Savta - *Grandmother*

Shalom - *Peace, often said as a greeting*

Synagogue - *Place of worship*

Yahweh - *God*

CODE BREAKER

Sam had a go at writing something using ancient Hebrew pictograph. As he couldn't find a symbol to use for God he decided to use letters, remembering what Rachel had once told him about Hebrew writing not having any vowels. Then he asked Kate if she could work it out. It took her a while but she got there in the end!

Do you remember what Shadrach said about reading the symbols being the easy part? Turning it into a story is more difficult. Can you do it?

Kate's answer is after the Bible References page. Try not to look unless you are really stuck!

These bible references will give you some clues (if you do not own a bible you can find them on the internet).

Mark ch 4 verses 26-29
1 Chronicles ch 16 verse 34
Psalm 69 verse 30
Deuteronomy ch 8 verse 10

Yhwh

Quick tip ... Symbols used more than once may have different meanings!

ANCIENT HEBREW PICTOGRAPH

	Aleph	Strong, Power, Leader	A
	Beyt	Family, House, In	B
	Gimel	Gather, Walk	G
	Dalet	Move, Hang, Entrance	D
	Hey	Look, Reveal, Breath	H
	Vav	Add, Secure, Hook	W
	Zayin	Food, Cut, Nourish	Z
	Chet	Wall, Outside, Divide, Half	Hh
	Tet	Surround, Contain, Mud	Th
	Yud	Hand, Work, Throw, Worship	Y
	Kaph	Bend, Open, Allow, Tame	K
	Lamed	Teach, Yoke, Authority, Bind	L

Ancient Hebrew Pictograph Cont.

ᎳᎳ	Mem	Water, Chaos, Mighty, Blood	M
	Nun	Seed, Continue, Heir, Son	N
	Samech	Grab, Hate, Protect	S
	Ayin	See, Watch, Know, Shade	Gh
	Pey	Open, Blow, Scatter, Edge	P
	Tsade	Trail, Journey, Chase, Hunt	Ts
	Quph	Condense, Circle, Time	Q
	Resh	Head, First, Top, Beginning	R
	Shin	Sharp, Press, Eat, Two	Sh
	Tav	Mark, Sign, Signal, Monument	T

BIBLE REFERENCES

If you would like to read about the events and places that Sam visited you will find them in the Christian bible. There are lots of different translations but one of the easiest to understand is the Good News Bible.

Old Testament Stories
    King Uzziah – *2 Chronicles ch 26*
    Naaman – *2 Kings ch 5*

New Testament Stories
    Lame man – *Mark ch 2 vs 1 - 12*
    Lepers – *Luke ch 17 vs 11 - 19*
    Women & children – *Matthew ch19 vs 13 – 15*
    Jesus' father – *Luke ch 1 vs 26 – 37*

KATE'S ANSWER

Scatter (sow?) the seed, water it then watch (wait?). When it's time, gather (reap?) the food (harvest?) and nourish (feed?) your family. Worship (give thanks to?) God as you eat.

Kate thought that the words in brackets would probably be the right ones to use in the language we speak today. Her story in today's language goes like this...

Sow the seed, water it then wait. When it's time, reap the harvest and feed your family. Give thanks to God as you eat.

Well done if your story is similar to Kate's!

Remember, your story doesn't have to match Kate's exactly but it should have the same meaning.

LEPROSY (HANSEN'S DISEASE)

Although Sam didn't know anything about leprosy it is still around today. It mainly affects people who live in countries like Africa and Asia.

It is not as contagious as it was thought in Bible times although a cure was not found until as recently as 1982. Even so, the disease must be treated as soon as possible to prevent people from becoming crippled. It can also result in blindness.

If you would like to find out more about the illness, the people it affects and the people who help them ask your teacher, parent or guardian.

Two good websites are at the bottom of the page but do get permission from your responsible adult first.

www.leprosymission.org.uk
www.lepra.org.uk

THANKS!

Thank you Martin for listening to each chapter more times than you would probably like! Thanks for all your suggestions, your support and encouragement, and your patience when I struggle with technology!

Thank you to all those who have prayed for me - this has been the hardest to write so far. God is our loving father who cares about every aspect of our lives but he is also holy and righteous and we must never forget that.

Thanks as always to Jesus for his wonderful inspiration, without which there would be no Sam and no opportunity to join his travels!

I hope you have enjoyed these adventures and will continue to share in Sam's journey as he learns more about God and how much he is loved.

ABOUT THE AUTHOR

Gill Parkes

Gill lives in Norfolk with her husband where she enjoys walks along the beach and exploring the countryside. She loves to spend time with her grandchildren, especially snuggling up with them to share a good book.

Jesus is her best friend and she hopes that by reading these stories you will get to know him too.

At the time of writing the world is experiencing the effects of Covid-19. Gill does not believe that God has inflicted this on us but she does believe He will use it to reveal himself and draw people to him. She has been working as a vaccinator as part of the team to help fight the global pandemic. It is her hope that God will use this to help bring healing to our world.

SAM PARROW'S TIME TRAVEL ADVENTURES

Sam Parrow And The Time Stone To Bethlehem

Sam Parrow Back In Time For Dinner

Sam Parrow And The Time Stone Secret

Look out for Sam's fourth time travel adventure when Sam helps look after the animals on the ark and learns the reason we have so many different languages!

BOOKS BY THIS AUTHOR

Sam Parrow And The Time Stone To Bethlehem

Bullied at school, Sam is transported back to the past where he makes new friends, learns about God's love and finds out just how much he is valued.

Sam Parrow Back In Time For Dinner

Sam realises there is more to God than he first thought as he and his friends join the Exodus, go to a wedding and learn how to give thanks when everything seems to be going wrong.

Printed in Great Britain
by Amazon